Buzz's Space Adventure

By Apple Jordan

Illustrated by Federico Mancuso, Giorgio Vallorani, and Jeff Jenney

Random House 🏠 New York

Published in the United States by Random House Children's Books, a division of Random House, Inc.,
1745 Broadway, New York, NY 10019, and in Canada by Random House of Canada Limited, Toronto, in conjunction with
Disney Enterprises, Inc. Random House and the colophon are registered trademarks of Random House, Inc.
randomhouse.com/kids
ISBN: 978-0-7364-2899-6
MANUFACTURED IN CHINA
10 9 8 7 6 5 4 3 2 1

One night, the Peas-in-a-Pod couldn't sleep. They asked Buzz Lightyear to tell them a story about space rangers.

Woody and Rex asked if they could be in the story, too.

"Sure!" said Buzz. He began a story about a special mission he was called on, once upon a time. . . .

The evil Emperor Zurg had stolen a top-secret space ranger turbo suit. Buzz had to find the suit and bring it home.

He asked two friends, First Lieutenant Woody and Second Lieutenant Rex, for help. Together they set off in their spaceship for Planet Zurg.

As the space rangers began to explore the rocky gray planet, they heard a strange humming sound.

Buzz and his crew looked over the edge of a huge canyon and saw hundreds of Zurgbots—soldiers in Emperor Zurg's army.

The Zurgbots spotted the space rangers and rushed toward them.

"We've got this covered, Captain!" cried Woody. While he and Rex fought off the Zurgbots, Buzz went on in search of Zurg.

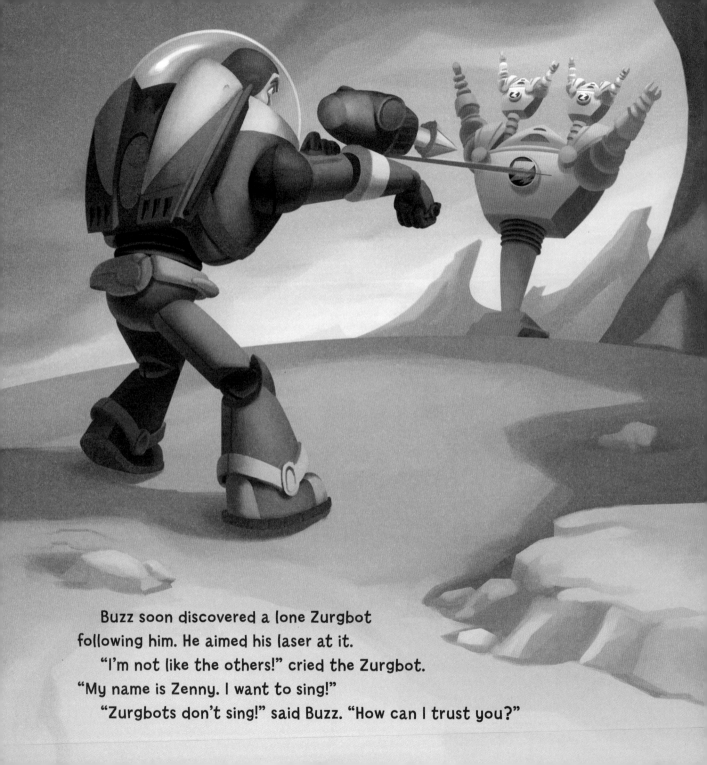

Buzz soon discovered a lone Zurgbot
following him. He aimed his laser at it.
"I'm not like the others!" cried the Zurgbot.
"My name is Zenny. I want to sing!"
"Zurgbots don't sing!" said Buzz. "How can I trust you?"

To prove he was trustworthy, Zenny led Buzz to Zurg's cave. They crept inside. There was the turbo suit!

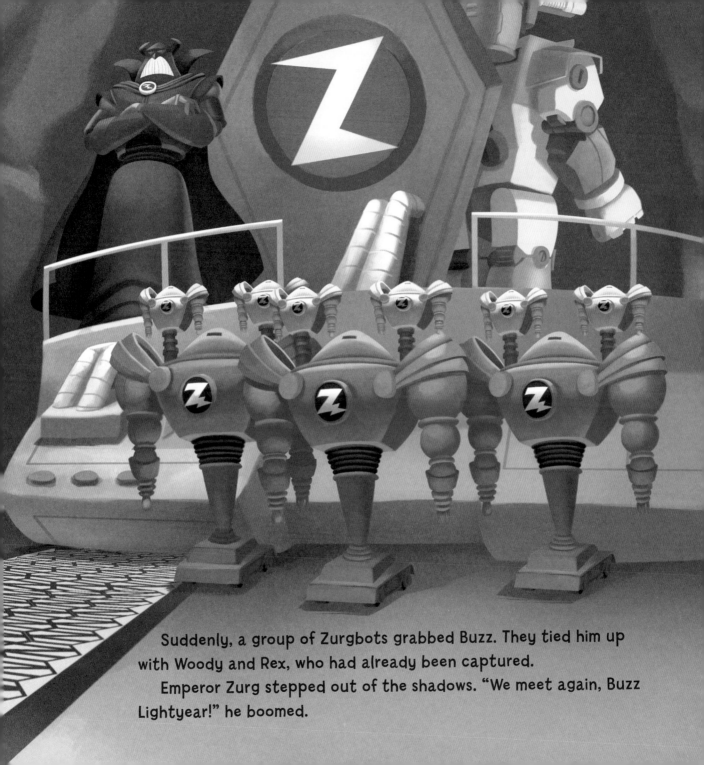

Suddenly, a group of Zurgbots grabbed Buzz. They tied him up with Woody and Rex, who had already been captured.

Emperor Zurg stepped out of the shadows. "We meet again, Buzz Lightyear!" he boomed.

"Not so fast, Zurg!" called a voice from the crowd. It was Zenny! He began to sing. Zenny really *was* different from the other Zurgbots.

As Zenny's voice grew louder and louder, stalactites on the cave's ceiling began falling to the floor, creating a cage around Zurg. He was trapped!

"Seize him!" Zurg cried to his Zurgbots.

Zenny quickly freed Buzz, Woody, and Rex.
Buzz raced over to the turbo suit and climbed inside. Now his space ranger powers were even greater! Turbo Buzz, Woody, Rex, and Zenny bravely battled the Zurgbots.

Soon Buzz and his crew had
defeated all the Zurgbots. They
thanked Zenny and returned to their
spaceship. Woody and Rex locked Zurg
into one of the ship's holding cells,
and Buzz stowed the turbo suit safely
away. Then they prepared for takeoff.

As the spaceship blasted off, Buzz saw Zenny on the ground below. He was teaching the other Zurgbots to sing!

Suddenly, the planet began to change. The gloomy caves and cliffs crumbled, and flowers and trees began to grow.

"Thanks to Zenny and his new friends," Buzz said, finishing his story, "Planet Zurg became a beautiful place."

And thanks to Buzz Lightyear, the Peas-in-a-Pod were fast asleep.

The toys let out a cheer and tossed Ken
into the air to celebrate their victory.
    "You're a great soldier, Ken," said Buzz.
    Sarge looked out at his troops with pride.
"Mission accomplished," he said.

Ken pulled Rex off the playhouse. The dinosaur sailed off the roof,
bounced off Stretch, and landed safely in the sandbox.

"That wasn't scary at all," said Rex. "It was fun!"

Suddenly, Ken had an idea.
"Stretch, hand me the 1972 cherry-red-striped platform boots!" he yelled.

Stretch threw the boots to Ken. After Ken put them on, he was tall enough to grab Rex!

"We need your help, soldier," Buzz said to Ken.

Ken looked at his boots. Then he looked
at Rex. Ken knew his friend needed him, so he
removed his boots and climbed to the top of
the tower. But it still wasn't tall enough.

The toys had to rescue Rex! Sarge and Buzz came up with a plan. Everyone agreed to help—except Ken. He didn't want to get his boots dirty.

The toys climbed onto each other's shoulders to build a toy tower. But the tower wasn't tall enough to reach Rex.

The moment Big Baby stopped rocking, Rex was launched off the truck—and onto the roof of the playhouse!

"Ahhh!" he cried as he flew through the air. The ground seemed so far away!

"On to the bouncy trucks!" commanded Sarge. "Move!"

Rex hopped onto one of the playground's bouncy trucks. Big Baby climbed on behind him and began to rock it back and forth.

"Too fast!" cried Rex. "Stop!"

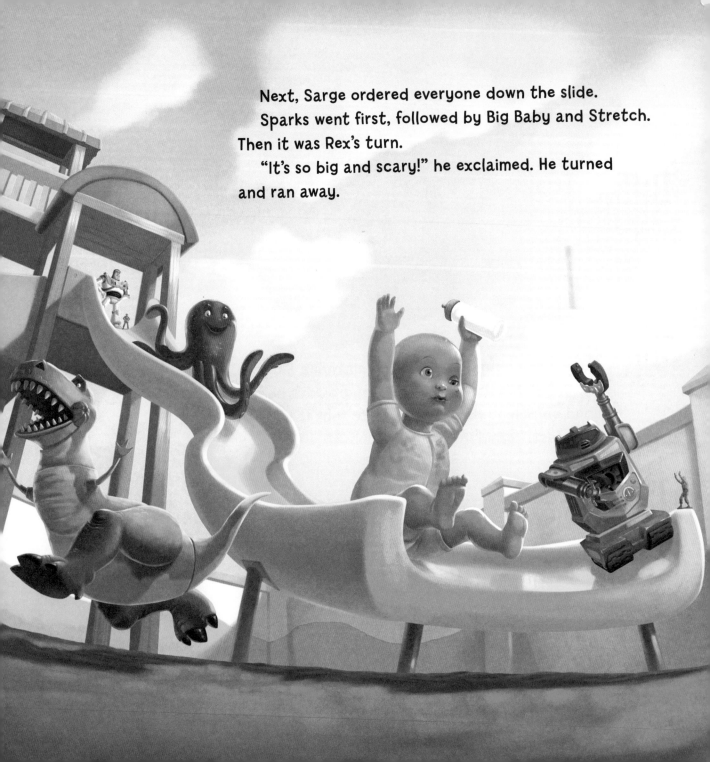

Next, Sarge ordered everyone down the slide.

Sparks went first, followed by Big Baby and Stretch.
Then it was Rex's turn.

"It's so big and scary!" he exclaimed. He turned
and ran away.

The rest of the toys were working hard. Chunk was pushing a heavy pile of blocks.

Sparks was doing some stretching exercises with a rubber band.

And Rex was leaping over hurdles—or at least, trying to.

Soon Ken returned wearing a new outfit
and carrying several boxes of boots.

"Take a few laps around the yard!" ordered Sarge.
"These boots weren't made for running!" cried Ken.

"Start training, soldiers!" ordered Sarge.
The toys began to lift weights. It was easy for
Stretch and Big Baby. But not for Rex.
"It's too heavy!" he cried.

"I have lots of boots in my closet!" exclaimed Ken.
He ran off to change his shoes before anyone could explain
that boot camp was training for soldiers, not a camp for boots.
     All the other toys were excited—except Rex. He was very nervous.

Buzz greeted Sarge, the Green Army Man who had found a home at Sunnyside. Sarge told Buzz he needed more soldiers. "Let's start a boot camp!" said Buzz.

One morning, Buzz and Rex climbed into Bonnie's backpack and went to Sunnyside Daycare to visit their friends.

SUNNYSIDE BOOT CAMP

By Annie Auerbach

Illustrated by the Disney Storybook Artists

Random House 🏠 New York

Published in the United States by Random House Children's Books, a division of Random House, Inc.,
1745 Broadway, New York, NY 10019, and in Canada by Random House of Canada Limited, Toronto, in conjunction
with Disney Enterprises, Inc. Random House and the colophon are registered trademarks of Random House, Inc.
randomhouse.com/kids
ISBN: 978-0-7364-2899-6
MANUFACTURED IN CHINA
10 9 8 7 6 5 4 3 2 1